ANIMAL LIFE

A Piccolo Factbook

Contents

ANIMAL LIFE

By David Lambert

Editor: Jacqui Bailey

Series Design: David Jefferis

A Piccolo Factbook

Staying Alive

There are more than a million kinds of living animal. Most are insects or other lowly beasts without a backbone. Only about 50,000 kinds of creature have a backbone. They include 30,000 kinds of fish and 9000 kinds of bird. There are also 5200 reptiles, such as snakes and lizards; 4000 mammals, such as kangaroos, cows and man; and 3200 amphibians, including frogs and salamanders.

Animals come in all sizes from amoeba, a blob of jelly almost too small to be seen, to the blue whale. A female blue whale with her unborn young may weigh as much as 35 bull elephants like the charging one shown here.

Creatures also come in many shapes and colours. But however large, small, or strangely shaped an animal may be, its body fits it for the way it lives.

Eaters and Eaten

All animals need food to fuel and build their bodies.
Unlike green plants they cannot make food from simple sub-
stances in air and water. They must get food ready-made
by eating plants or other animals. The nourishment in
leaves is so low that cows spend hours grazing every day.

But a big meat meal lasts a lion several days and could keep a python alive for several months.

Food Chains
Every creature is a link in a chain of eaters and eaten. In a wood, insects eat leaves; warblers eat insects; hawks eat warblers. Each wood, pond and meadow has its food chains that criss-cross to form a food web—a web of life.

Food Pyramids
Food chains also build food pyramids. In each pyramid a meat-eater needs to eat more than its own weight of plant-eaters, who need to eat more than their weight of plants.

Creatures near the bottom of a pyramid are smaller and more plentiful than those at the top. In a stretch of Arizona desert scientists counted 17,948 mice and other rodents, yet only one coyote and two birds of prey.

Small plant-eating creatures breed far faster than beasts that prey upon them. If nothing stopped it, a tiny jelly-like protozoan could produce enough descendants in one week to outweigh the Earth.

Nourishment is passed on and on. A falcon kills a redstart that ate caterpillars that ate green leaves. Soil bacteria and fungi turn fallen leaves into nourishment that tree roots use to make new leaves.

9

Claws and Fangs

Most plant-eating animals have no problems getting food. Plants obligingly stay put while the creatures browse or graze upon them. Obtaining food is harder for predators, beasts that prey on other animals, for these may run away or fight back. But, just as many plant-eaters have teeth designed to crop and grind leaves, so the hunters have built-in weapons which help them catch and kill their victims.

Stabbing and Cutting

Many predators have weapons that can stab or cut. Cats have sharp teeth and claws, but no living cat can match *Smilodon's* weapons. The dagger-like teeth of this prehistoric sabretooth cat could pierce an elephant's thick hide.

Birds of prey attack with powerful talons and a beak hooked for tearing flesh. But one fishing bird, the darter, uses its long sharp bill like a spear.

Among fishes, a shoal of small but sharp-toothed piranhas can strip a human body to bones in minutes.

The Poisoners

Jellyfish, scorpions, and certain spiders, snakes and insects kill or paralyze by poison. Some poisons make the victim bleed inside. Others stop it breathing.

When a snake bites, the poison is squirted through its two hollow teeth into its victim. A wasp injects poison through its sting.

Setting Traps

Some hunters catch their prey with traps. The angler fish snaps up small fish, which are attracted by a fleshy lure growing from its head. The ant-lion larva digs a pit in sand and waits inside for ants that tumble into it.

Leopards are fierce and strong enough to kill an antelope and haul it out of reach of other animals.

11

Defence

Fast, long-legged beasts can run from an attacker. But some peaceful animals fight back if threatened. A zebra or an ostrich can give a powerful kick. Porcupines jab spines into an enemy.

A few animals keep still and depend on body armour for protection. A tortoise pulls its head and legs inside its shell. A pangolin (or scaly anteater) has hard scales that guard its body when it rolls up in a ball.

Chemical Weapons

Some creatures' best defence is their unpleasant taste or smell. Skunks squirt a stinking fluid at attackers. Beasts that bite a salamander will find that it has poison in its skin.

Like the black and yellow fire salamander, bees and wasps are brightly coloured to warn their enemies that attacking them is dangerous.

Defence by Trickery

Harmless hoverflies resemble bees so closely that many creatures will not eat them for fear of being stung. This kind of defence by imitating other animals is called *mimicry*.

Many animals try to make themselves invisible. Some burrow. Others keep still and their shapes or colours allow them to blend into their surroundings. A plaice can even change colour to match the sea bed below it.

Bluff can often fool an enemy. Squid squirt a cloud of ink to confuse an attacker. Toads puff themselves up to seem larger than they are. A threatened grass snake pretends to be dead until its enemy grows bored and simply wanders off.

Australia's frilled lizard scares enemies by spreading out the large collar of skin around its neck. Its ruff is held up by 'ribs' that jut from its tongue bone. These spread apart when it opens its mouth wide.

The moth (right) and the grasshopper (above) cling to backgrounds that match their own colours. If they keep still, their enemies will not discover them.

Scroungers

Animals and plants are always dying. Yet you seldom see dead wild animals; and dead plants disappear in time. All are cleared away by nature's dustmen. Instead of eating living animals or plants these creatures eat dead flesh, droppings, rotting wood or fallen leaves.

Carrion Eaters

Some birds and mammals are well built for eating carrion—the flesh of beasts they find already dead. Vultures and marabou storks have naked heads and necks. They can plunge their beaks into a big corpse without

White-headed vultures wait for a zebra to die. Then they will eat it.

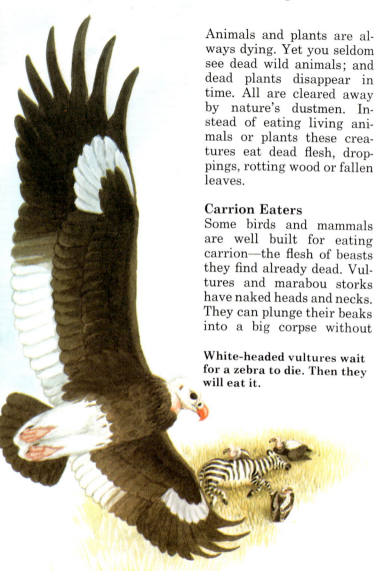

messing up their feathers. The spotted hyena has stronger jaws for its size than any other mammal. It can crack big bones to reach the nourishment inside.

Small Scavengers

Many beasts that eat dead plants or animals are tiny.

Some beetles tackle corpses far larger than themselves. Burying beetles dig away the soil beneath a dead bird or mouse. When it is buried a female beetle lays eggs beside it. When the grubs hatch they eat the corpse.

The wood of rotting tree trunks and branches provides a larder for certain kinds of beetles, as well as for millipedes and woodlice.

But hundreds of kinds of beetle prefer their food at second hand. These beetles eat dung dropped on the ground by grazing animals.

Dung beetles roll dung into a ball. Then they bury it as a food store for their own young.

A hyena eats the remains of a large beast killed by a lion. But hyenas also kill their own prey.

Super Senses

All animals have senses to help them stay alive. In some animals, certain senses are amazingly acute.

Eyes and Ears
Vultures have keen eyesight. A vulture soaring thousands of metres high can see a dead horse far below. Like man, monkeys have forward facing eyes that can focus on one object. This helps them to judge distance as they leap about in trees.

Owls and bats with long ears can pick up sounds as faint as a vole munching grass, or a moth in flight. Bats and dolphins can find

Sensitive feelers called barbels help this catfish to find food in the mud of the rivers or lakes where it lives. All fishes have a so-called lateral line down each side of the body. Here, special 'portholes' under the scales sense vibrations set up in water by fishes nearby.

their way about by making sounds and listening to the echoes bounced back from the objects around them.

Smell and Taste
Salmon have a fine sense of taste. When they swim in from the sea they can find by taste the water of the river where they hatched out years before. Taste is similar to smell. Some male moths have a sense of smell so keen that they can smell the scent of female moths about a kilometre away.

A fly's compound eye has over 4000 lenses. Each lens gives it a 'picture'. Such eyes are quick to detect any movement near them.

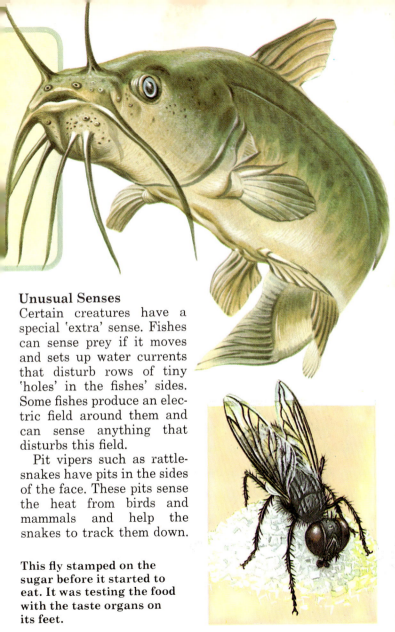

Unusual Senses

Certain creatures have a special 'extra' sense. Fishes can sense prey if it moves and sets up water currents that disturb rows of tiny 'holes' in the fishes' sides. Some fishes produce an electric field around them and can sense anything that disturbs this field.

Pit vipers such as rattle-snakes have pits in the sides of the face. These pits sense the heat from birds and mammals and help the snakes to track them down.

This fly stamped on the sugar before it started to eat. It was testing the food with the taste organs on its feet.

How Animals Move

Most creatures must be able to move about to find food or mates or to escape from their enemies. To travel forward they push back against the ground or air or water.

Travelling on Land
Many thousand kinds of animals push with legs that work as levers. Man has only two legs, but some millipedes have 700. Most creatures use their legs to walk or run, but some are expert jumpers. A flea can leap 130 times its own height. If it were a man this would be like jumping higher than St Paul's Cathedral in London.

Some legless creatures travel well on the ground. Snakes wriggle along by pressing back against roughnesses in the ground. Big snakes can crawl in a straight line, using their belly scales to press down and backward.

When a flying squirrel leaps from a high branch, flaps of skin between its front and back legs become parachutes that help the animal to glide slowly down.

The fish (opposite) uses fins to swim. The spider (left) has legs, and the butterfly, wings.

Travelling in Air and Water

Fishes swim by pushing water backward with the tail and body. Insects called water boatmen use long, hairy legs as oars to row them through the water. Some tiny one-celled creatures lash themselves along with little whip-like hairs. Scallops and squids are jet propelled. If threatened, they can shoot forward by squirting water backwards.

Birds and bats have wings. They use them to push back on the air and move themselves forwards and up. Some frogs, fish and squirrels are also said to fly. In fact these only glide. They cannot gain height in the air.

Spiders cannot fly, yet tiny spiders may drift high and far above the ground. Spiders spin threads so light that the wind lifts the threads and spiders up into the air. Spiders have drifted out to sea and come down on ships 300 kilometres from land.

Bristles jutting from its skin help a worm to get a grip on soil.

19

Animal Travellers

Each year millions of animals make long journeys called migrations. Migrating animals travel far to find food or breeding grounds or to escape the winter cold.

Land Travellers

When winter comes, herds of caribou and reindeer leave the treeless Arctic and find food and shelter in forests farther south. East African herds of antelopes follow the rains that nourish the grasses they eat.

Air Travellers

Birds can migrate far farther than land animals. Each autumn at least 1000 million birds of more than 230 kinds leave Europe for Africa. Some fly almost half-way around the world, then back.

A small warbler can fly more than 1000 kilometres without a meal. It gets its energy by first storing fat in its body. The fat may weigh as much as the rest of the bird.

Ocean Voyagers

Eels from Europe and North Africa cross the Atlantic Ocean to spawn. Salmon swim inland from the sea to spawn in the same tiny stream where they were hatched. Each year grey whales may travel 22,000 kilometres. No other mammal migrates as far as that.

Below: Eels hatch in the Sargasso Sea (shown ringed). Some drift and swim to North America, others reach Europe and North Africa.

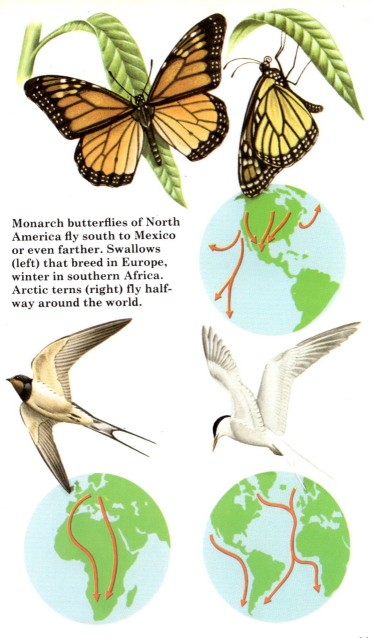

Monarch butterflies of North America fly south to Mexico or even farther. Swallows (left) that breed in Europe, winter in southern Africa. Arctic terns (right) fly half-way around the world.

The Long Sleep

Some animals spend cold winters in a deep sleep called hibernation. Hibernating creatures use so little energy that they can live for months without a meal. So sleeping saves the lives of animals whose food is scarce in winter.

Animals about to hibernate seek out some comfortable hole or crevice. Whole groups may hibernate together. As many as 800 of the poisonous snakes called adders have been found together sleeping underground.

When mammals hibernate their bodies grow cold blooded like those of snakes or frogs. This means they cool down or warm up like their surroundings. The body temperature

Snake

Dormouse

Toad

Tortoise

of a dormouse is usually 37°C. In hibernation its temperature may drop to an almost ice-cold 2°C. Hibernating creatures breathe so seldom and they have such slow heart beats that people sometimes think they are dead.

Living Larders

To stay alive a hibernating creature uses fat stored in its body. When hibernation starts the animal has stored so much fat that it is plump. When hibernation ends the fat is gone and the beast is thin and hungry. A ground squirrel may lose three-quarters of its weight in the foodless months. These last most of the year in Europe's far north. There, the common lizard feeds from June to August, then spends nine months sleeping underground.

These six animals are hibernating to escape winter cold and lack of food. The dormouse and hedgehog are both mammals. The snake and tortoise are reptiles. The toad and newt are amphibians. Most animals seek out frost-free crevices or holes. These are often underground. People have found snakes sleeping in the same hole as lizards they would usually eat. When the hunters settle down to hibernate they feel too dozy to attack.

The Shape Changers

Most creatures always have the same shape. But some change their shapes and way of life as they grow.

Strange Crustaceans

Crustaceans like crabs and barnacles begin as tiny spiky creatures that swim like water fleas. After several body changes a crab grows claws and tucks its tail beneath it. Then it settles on the sea bed.

Amazing Insects

Bees, beetles, butterflies and many more insects *metamorphose,* or change shape, as they grow.

Flies start life as fat white maggots. Many beetles start as grubs that live in wood. Some of the insects called cicadas live underground for 17 years before they grow their wings.

Fishy Freaks

Plaice hatch out as normal baby fishes. As each grows it becomes flattened from side to side. One eye moves around the head to join the other. Then the fish settles eye-side up on the sea bed.

Egg

Below: Frogspawn hatches into tadpoles. They lose their tails and gills, grow legs and lungs, and so turn into froglets.

Spawn

Tadpoles

Caterpillar

Red admiral butterfly

Chrysalis

Above: An egg hatches into a caterpillar. This eats leaves as it grows. In time it fastens onto a leaf. Its skin splits and reveals a chrysalis, which grows a hard shell. Days or months later, the shell splits and a fully grown butterfly crawls out.

Froglet

Egyptian plovers pick parasites from a Nile crocodile at rest on a river bank. The birds may even boldly step inside a crocodile's open mouth to eat leeches—parasitic worms living between the crocodile's teeth.

Living Side by Side

Most animals spend at least some time with others. Many only meet to breed. Others always live in groups of their own kind. Some animals share their lives with creatures of a different kind.

Partners and Parasites

Certain creatures benefit from providing others with protection or food. A hermit crab will place a sea anemone on the empty shell the crab has made its home. The sea anemone stings the crab's enemies, and the crab carries the sea anemone to new feeding grounds. Small fishes called wrasses eat parasites that live and feed on larger fishes. In this way the wrasses find food, and the other fishes are made comfortable. Similarly, tick birds eat the ticks that burrow in the hides of African buffaloes and rhinoceroses. Birds and hosts all benefit by this behaviour.

Various creatures have become specially shaped for life with others. Remoras are fishes with suckers which they use to cling onto sharks to hitch a ride. Fleas are insects that are flattened from side to side. They can hop easily between the hairs on mammals. Feather lice are flat from top to bottom. This helps them creep between birds' feathers.

Flocks, Herds and Packs

Herds of up to ten million antelopes once roamed south-western Africa. Twice that many bats roost in one cave in Texas. A swarm of locusts may consist of 250,000 million insects. Migrating starlings fly in flocks that number tens of thousands. Anchovetas are small fishes that shoal in billions off Peru.

It pays such animals to travel, feed, or breed together in large numbers. One reason is that predators find it difficult to single out and attack one individual in a flock or herd. Also, if one member of a herd finds food the rest will follow it and find food too.

Wildebeeste are large antelopes that graze and roam in herds across African grasslands. At least some members of a herd will see a lion creeping nearby. Any lion leaping at a herd risks being trampled by scores of hooves or jabbed by many horns.

Some groups are kept together by a powerful 'boss'. In a troop of baboons each member has its rank. The most powerful males travel in the middle with the females and young. Less powerful males guard the front and rear.

Hunting as a Team

One wolf could not kill a caribou. One wild dog or hyena could not kill a zebra. Yet wolves, hyenas and wild dogs do hunt and kill grazing animals that are far larger than themselves. This is possible because these hunters work in packs. First they separate a weak individual from a herd. Next they chase the animal until it tires. Then they close in and pull the victim down. Many fangs make short work of any zebra, antelope or deer.

Musk oxen live in herds on cold, treeless Arctic lands called *tundra*. If wolves appear, adult musk oxen gather in an outward-facing ring, with the young protected in the middle. Bulls always face the enemy.

Insect Cities

The most amazing animals that live in groups are those that dwell in cities built of mud or wax or paper. These creatures are ants, termites, and some kinds of bees and wasps.

Just like human city dwellers, each insect performs a particular task that helps to keep its city working. Yet, unlike people, the insects do not learn their tasks. They work automatically, by instinct.

How Ants Live

Many of the 15,000 kinds of ant build their nests in the ground. A nest usually has several large female ants called queens. Their task is simply laying eggs. One queen may lay 30,000 eggs every few weeks for 10 years or more. Male ants simply fertilize the queen, then die. Females not fertilized become workers. Some feed young ants and queens. Others find food. Workers with big jaws act as soldiers. Their job is to protect the colony from attack.

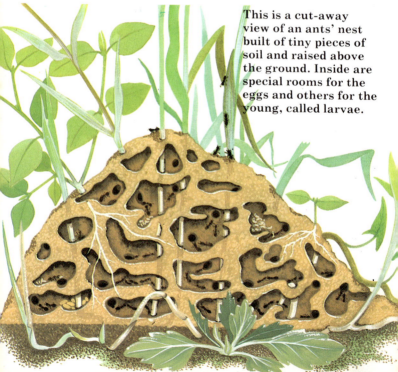

This is a cut-away view of an ants' nest built of tiny pieces of soil and raised above the ground. Inside are special rooms for the eggs and others for the young, called larvae.

Wild honeybees tend a nest on a branch. Its waxy cells hold the eggs, larvae, pollen and honey, which are all looked after by the worker bees.

Termites

Termites tend to look like white ants. As many as two million may live inside a mud pillar built higher than a small house. Usually a nest has one queen, one king and thousands of workers and soldiers who do not breed.

The Honeybee

Up to 50,000 honeybees may live inside one hive. Its queen came from a larva fed on special food called royal jelly. Other females act as workers. They produce wax to build the honeycomb. They gather pollen and nectar and make honey. A bee may visit 1500 clover blossoms to fill its honey stomach. To make a pot of honey one bee would have to fly a distance equal to that of three times around the world.

Male bees are known as drones. They fertilize young queens. Workers let drones starve to death in autumn when food grows scarce and their usefulness is over.

31

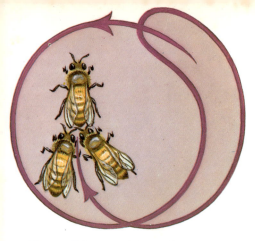

Bees pass messages to one another by performing special 'dances'. A bee that dances in a circle over the hive tells the others it has found food nearby. A dance done in a special direction shows the other bees which way to fly to find the food.

Sending Signals

Animals send signals for several reasons. One is just to keep in touch with animals of their own kind. Migrating birds that fly by night call to keep their flock together. Rabbits thump their feet and pheasants squawk to warn of danger. But signals can also be threatening.

Warning: Keep Away!
Many animals have a home ground where they live and feed. If one fox's home ground is invaded by other foxes there may be too little food for all of them. The first fox signals others to keep out by leaving droppings around the edge of his own territory. Many mammals use scent to mark their home ground in such ways. Cats spray urine. Hippopotamuses use dung. Antelopes smear twigs with scent from glands on their faces. Male birds tend to warn off others of their own kind by singing.

If a creature strays into another's territory, the owner will threaten the invader. A male green lizard hunches his shoulders, lowers his head and walks jerkily toward the enemy. A fiddler crab waves his larger claw about. A cichlid fish opens his fins and flaps his tail at the intruder. A black-headed gull holds his neck up, points his beak down and slightly lifts his wings.

Giving in Gracefully

Most invading or weaker animals give in rather than risk a fight. To show that they submit they use a special set of signals. A black-headed gull turns his beak aside. A dog offers his neck to his rival. A cichlid closes his fins and tail. A lizard pats the ground with her feet.

One creature's submission signals usually weaken the other's urge to fight. But some home owners still insist on driving the intruder off their territory.

If two wolves meet, the weaker one may cower and lie down leaving its throat open to attack. This tells the stronger wolf that the other does not want to fight.

Meeting a Mate

To produce young, most females must first mate with males of their own kind. Many creatures attract a mate with special signals that can be seen, smelt or heard.

Fireflies and female glow-worms glow in the dark. Male moths and fishes find females by following the scent they give off. Male grasshoppers make chirping sounds by rubbing their hind legs on their front wings. Birds and whales sing to say where they are. Deer bark or bellow.

Winning a Wife

When a male meets a female he may woo her with a special display. A male bird of paradise will hang upside down to show off his beautiful plumage. Some males build a nest to attract a hen bird. Male bowerbirds build 'huts' or avenues decorated with shells, flowers or pebbles and perhaps even painted with earth colours mixed with saliva.

Avoiding Aggression

Many creatures mistake a would-be mate for a meal or an enemy. But submission signals help to keep them from fighting. A male spider may offer a female a fly wrapped in his silk thread. A female cichlid flattens her fins against her sides.

Dancing brings some pairs together. Male and female great-crested grebes face one another as they rear up and crouch in the water.

Fights do happen. A female praying mantis will eat her husband as they mate. But most courtship battles are between rival male animals and few come to harm.

To court this peahen, the peacock spreads the lovely feathers above his tail and vibrates them until the colours shimmer.

Long-tailed tit

Woodpecker

Common
bowl-shaped
nest.

Tailorbird

Wren

Building a Home

The caddis worm glues stems or stones onto its soft body to protect it. The hermit crab creeps inside an empty sea shell. The mole rat digs tunnels that may stretch hundreds of metres underground. Like ants and bees, such creatures live inside their homes. But many animals build homes simply as somewhere safe to stay while they raise a family.

Birds' Nests

Birds build perhaps the most amazing nests of all. The smallest are those of the hummingbirds. Their tiny cups of lichen, moss and spiders' webs are little bigger than a thimble. The largest nests belong to the scrub-fowl of Australia. These nests are mounds,

Birds build nests in many ways and many places.

some are higher than a man. Inside it is hot enough for eggs to hatch.

Mammals' Homes

Rabbits, foxes, badgers and many other mammals raise their young in burrows. But some mammals build above the ground. Harvest mice weave ball-shaped nests of grass among stems one metre or more high. Muskrats seek safety in swamps. They pile plants into mounds Inside each mound is a nest.

Fishy Builders

Cichlids will simply clean a stone and lay eggs on it. But some fishes build nests. A male Siamese fighter builds a nursery of bubbles. Male sticklebacks make nests from bits of plant which they stick together with a special kind of glue.

A beaver's lodge is built of sticks and mud in the middle of a pool. Here, beavers can raise their young in safety.

Animal Families

The ocean sunfish lays as many as 300 million eggs. Because she simply sheds them in the sea very few survive to hatch. An elephant has just one baby at a time. Because she guards and feeds it, her baby has a good chance of growing up. Unlike the ocean sunfish, animals that care for their young can have fewer young to keep their kind alive.

Cold-blooded Parents
Most animals without backbones leave their young to fend for themselves. But a hunting wasp will lay her eggs on caterpillars she has stung and paralyzed. This gives her young fresh food when they hatch. Scorpions and some spiders carry their babies on their backs.

Some fishes guard their eggs with care. Seahorse babies hatch from eggs kept in a pouch in the father's belly. When her eggs hatch, a female Nile crocodile puts the babies inside her jaws and takes them to the safety of the water. Certain frogs begin as tadpoles swallowed by their father. They turn into froglets inside him. Then he spits them out.

Birds and Mammals
Birds will sit on their eggs for weeks to keep them warm so that they hatch. Then the parents work hard to feed their young. In 18 days a blue-tit family may eat 10,000 caterpillars.

Mammal mothers feed their babies with milk from special glands. Kangaroos and other marsupials (see p. 55) are so tiny and weak when they are born they need special care.

Below: A mouthbrooder and young. If danger threatens, the young fishes will swim inside their parent's mouth.

Above: A young koala clings to its mother's back. When it was born it lived safely inside a warm pouch in the mother's belly.

Below: Snuggled down on their mother's back, these merganser ducklings are safe from big fishes that might eat them.

Learning and Play

Playing active games not only makes our bodies stronger, it helps us learn what we can do. We learn which spaces we can squeeze into. We learn how far to jump to land across a ditch instead of in the middle. We learn, too, how to get on with other people.

It is the same with some wild mammals. Play helps their young to learn to cope with life. The picture above shows a badger family at play. Two youngsters grapple in a mock fight, while another learns that hedgehogs can be prickly. Many animal games seem like practice for catching prey or escaping predators. A kitten creeps up on a ball of wool and pounces as it would upon a mouse. Lambs race around a field as they would if chased by wolves.

Parents playing with their young sometimes seem to be teaching them to hunt. A cat will show her kittens how to

catch and kill a mouse. Yet scientists have found that untaught cats will hunt by instinct. So it may be that many of the games young mammals play are just instinctive ways of using up spare energy.

Adult Animals at Play

Few wild adult animals play games. Finding food takes all their energy. But otters have been seen to toss a pebble in a stream and dive in after it.

Captive adult animals have energy to spare. Some use it up and keep their bodies fit by play. Sea lions will toss a piece of wood about. Lions and elephants will roll a ball. Wild goats play king of the castle. A chimpanzee may squirt mouthfuls of water at passers-by.

Even birds are sometimes playful. Macaws will toy with stones. One parrot enjoyed being thrown up and caught. But ants and other animals that act only by instinct are unable to enjoy a game.

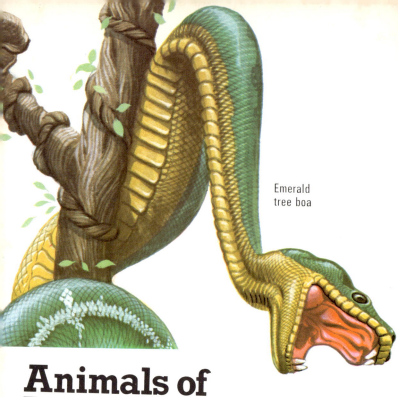
Emerald
tree boa

Animals of Land and Air

Some parts of the world are desert, others grassland. Snow
and ice cover huge stretches of the far north and far south.
Great mountain ranges cut across continents. Shady
forests sprawl over vast areas of the hot tropics and the
cool northern regions.

Most creatures living in each of these places thrive there
and nowhere else. The first part of this chapter looks at
different kinds of land and climate and how the animals
that live there fit in with their surroundings. The second
part of the chapter looks at some of the more unusual and
interesting backboned animals that walk on land or leap
into the air and fly.

Tropical Forest Animals

The warm rainy forests of the tropics always have trees that bear leaves, and flowers or fruits. So there is always food for creatures that can climb or fly.

Chimpanzee

Apes and monkeys use their grasping hands to swing and leap from branch to branch. Chimpanzees climb to gather fruit, though they prefer walking on the ground.

Snakes like the emerald tree boa shown here lie on the branches to ambush passing squirrels, birds or lizards.

Hummingbirds or sunbirds flit among the sunlit treetops sucking nectar from the blossoms. Eagles soar above the forest. Sometimes one plunges down to seize a lizard, bird or monkey.

Another set of creatures finds food on the dimly lit forest floor. Here wild pigs grub among the fallen leaves, and antelopes or tapirs browse upon the shrubs. Hunting them are jaguars or leopards. The dappled light falling on their spotted coats hides these big cats from their prey.

Northern Forest Life

The huge, needle-leaved forests of Canada and Russia hold less food than the tropical forests. The northern winter is long and cold. Yet some hardy mammals make their home among the pine and spruce trees. Little mouse-like voles and lemmings keep active all the winter. They find plant foods by burrowing beneath the snow. Up above, squirrels leap among the branches, where they feed on pine cones.

Bears are the north's most powerful hunters. But lynxes are among the fiercest. These large cats have ear tufts, and broad feet to help them walk in snow.

43

Prairie falcon

Grassland Animals

Grasslands stretch across large parts of the world. They are too dry to nourish many trees, so animals that live here must find food and safety in the wide open spaces.

Steppes and Prairies
Just south of the great northern forests are rather dry regions covered with short grasses. These lands are the steppes of Asia and the prairies of North America.

Here, grass is what most mammals eat. Many are rodents. They have sharp chisel-shaped front teeth that help them chop off the plant stems. Their cheek teeth grind the grass to pulp. Grass-eating rodents such as voles must eat large, frequent meals, for there is little nourishment in grass.

The grass-eaters have another problem: where to hide from their enemies. Rodents, such as prairie dogs, dig burrows where they raise their families. Mole rats eat roots and never leave their holes. Hares and the large grazers, the antelopes and bison, simply run away.

For the burrowers, danger comes from beasts like badgers and foxes that try to dig them out, or eagles that swoop down from the sky.

Tropical Grasslands

Tall grasses help to hide many of the creatures living in the savanna grasslands of the tropics.

Herds of zebras, antelopes, giraffes and others roam the African savanna. Some of these animals eat nothing except grass, while other kinds browse on shrubs or scattered trees. In this way there is enough food for all.

In turn, some of the plant-eaters are food for the big cats like leopards, lions and cheetahs. Cheetahs can outrun the fastest antelope. Meat left over by the hunters is soon snapped up by vultures, jackals and hyenas.

North American prairie animals: (1) badger; (2) bison fighting; (3) prairie dogs in and near their burrow; (4) prairie chicken; (5) pronghorns looking out for danger; (6) pocket gopher by its hole; (7) coyote prowling.

Mountaineers

Thin air, cold winds, and cliffs make life difficult and dangerous for animals whose homes are high among the mountains of the world.

Yet up here they have grass to eat and they are safe from attack by the hunting beasts that roam the plains below.

But only agile creatures can survive among the steep slopes and pinnacles. Wild sheep, wild goats and chamois have hooves that grip like climbing boots. The hooves help their owners leap up cliffs from ledge to ledge. Springy heels allow a chamois to land safely after plunging nine metres from one rock to another lower down.

Climbing creatures use a lot of oxygen from the air they breathe. Big lungs help them to get enough oxygen from the thin mountain air. A drop of a vicuna's blood is three times richer in oxygen than a drop of human blood.

Thick fur or hair helps to keep the animals warm in the bitterly cold winds. Rocky Mountain goats also have thick fat and a thick hide that helps to trap more heat.

Chamois

The Andean condor soars over the Andes mountains of South America in search of dead animals. This vulture is one of the largest of all birds that are able to fly.

Below are three sure-footed, hoofed mammals that live among the mountains. The chamois and mouflon live on mountainsides in Europe. The vicuna roams Andean grasslands. Thick, soft hair helps to keep it warm.

Vicuna

Mouflon

Surviving Snow and Ice

The lands of the far north and far south are the harshest anywhere on Earth. Winters are long, dark, and very, very cold. Snow or ice cover the ground for many months.

Most of Antarctica is always frozen. Seals and penguins land on this southern continent to breed. But no backboned animal finds enough food to live here all year round. Only tiny mites and insects manage that.

Living in the Arctic

In the north, plants thrive in the short Arctic summer. Food is plentiful and thousands of ducks and geese fly in from southern lands to raise their families. The little mouse-like lemmings multiply. Then comes autumn. Snow falls, food gets hard to find, and most birds fly away.

Snowy owl

Arctic hare

These Arctic animals can keep warm among ice or snow. Thick hair or fur trap body heat for the hare, fox, lemmings, and polar bear. The seal and walrus have a thick layer of protective fat beneath their skins. The short ears of the Arctic hare and Arctic fox lose less heat than the long ears of hares and foxes in hotter countries.

Lemmings

Arctic fox

Polar bear

Walrus

Harp seal

Yet Arctic animals survive the winter. Lemmings eat plants stored in their burrows tunnelled under the snow. It can be 22°C warmer down there than up above. Arctic hares nibble plants on snow-free slopes. Foxes and snowy owls hunt hares or lemmings. Polar bears prowl the frozen sea. They kill seals coming up to breathe at holes kept open in the ice. Thick fur or feathers help to keep Arctic creatures warm. Some are coloured white and match the snow. This hides them from their enemies.

Life Without Water

Parts of Africa, Asia, Australia and the Americas are hot, dry deserts. By day the ground can be too hot to touch, yet at night it may be almost freezing. Rain seldom falls and pools and streams usually lie empty. Plants grow only here and there among the stones or sand. The plants have tough leaves or spines.

Hot deserts are so harsh, explorers have died crossing them. Yet for many creatures they are comfortable homes.

Saving Water

Some desert creatures never drink. They get water from the juices in the plants or animals they eat. Some small rodents find enough moisture in dry seeds, and sand rats can eat salty leaves.

Desert creatures store water in their bodies in various ways. Waterproof skins help reptiles to keep in moisture. An American tortoise stores water in its bladder. Camels lose little water as urine, and sweat only when they become very hot indeed. A camel can lose almost one-third of its weight in water without dying.

Travelling on Sand
Many creatures find it difficult to walk on sand. But the camel's spreading feet help to stop it sinking in. Sidewinder rattlesnakes cross sand with a special sideways kind of wriggle.

Beating the Heat
Some deserts are hot enough by day to fry an egg on the ground. To stop their bodies burning, some desert lizards stand on tiptoe and hold each leg in turn off the ground. Rodents and snakes escape the heat by hiding in burrows. The long legs and ears of animals like desert antelopes act as radiators that give off body heat and help to keep their owners cool.

As dusk falls the land cools down and desert burrowers creep out to feed.

Creatures feed at dusk in a desert in south-western North America. Kangaroo rats (1) are hunted by a rattlesnake (2). The scorpion (3) and collared lizard (4) are insect eaters. The jackrabbit (5) feeds on plants, and is hunted by predators such as lynxes and kit foxes.

51

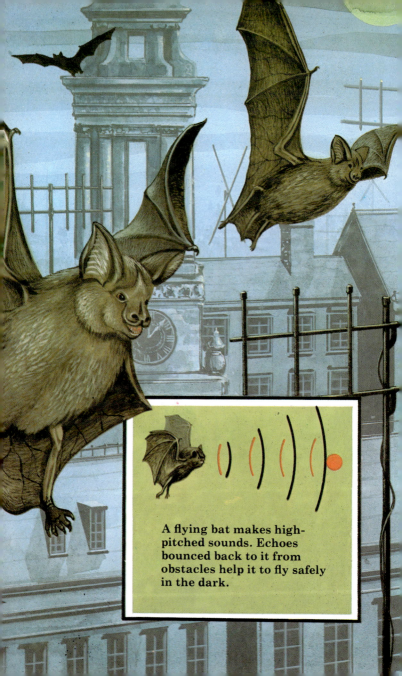

A flying bat makes high-pitched sounds. Echoes bounced back to it from obstacles help it to fly safely in the dark.

Life in the Dark

In most parts of the world certain creatures are active only at night or underground. Such animals find food and avoid enemies where it is far too dark for us to see.

Life at Night
Creatures that come out at night have senses that guide or warn them in the gloom.

Many rodents and insect-eating mammals have weak eyes but a keen sense of smell.

Cats largely hunt at night by sound and smell. Also a cat's whiskers help it to feel its way through undergrowth. Once it creeps near its prey the cat can see it, even if the light is very dim. For its size, a cat has larger eyes than any other flesh-eating mammal.

But even cats cannot imitate the Cuban boa. This snake hunts bats in dark caves. It finds them by their body heat and can even catch a bat as it flies by.

Bats and owls are well designed to fly at night. An owl's eyes may be ten times more sensitive to light than ours. Soft feathers help owls to fly without a sound.

Bats with weak eyes can navigate by sound. For instance a fish-eating bat flies above the water making clicking sounds. Echoes tell the bat where a fish lies just below the surface. As the bat flies by it lowers its hind claws and grabs the fish.

Life Underground
Some creatures spend their lives in caves or burrows where no light ever reaches. Such beasts have very tiny eyes or none at all, and most are blind.

Blind white fishes and salamanders swim in certain caves, finding food by smell.

Moles dig with hands like little spades as they burrow after worms. Their fur is so thick that the soil around them cannot cling.

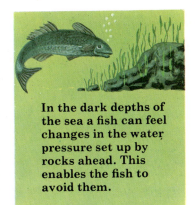

In the dark depths of the sea a fish can feel changes in the water pressure set up by rocks ahead. This enables the fish to avoid them.

Strange Land Animals

Australia's rat kangaroo is a marsupial, but it looks very like the un-pouched kangaroo rat found on other continents.

The Komodo dragon is an Indonesian lizard large enough to kill and eat pigs, deer and monkeys.

When European travellers reached other continents they found creatures unlike any they had ever seen.

South America has strange climbing beasts called sloths. These mammals climb slowly upside down among the branches. They can scarcely crawl if put on the ground.

Africa has the aardvark, a creature rather like a pig with donkey's ears and a tube-shaped face. Aardvarks tear open termite nests and use their long sticky tongues to catch the insects.

In a few South-East Asian islands lives the Komodo dragon, the largest lizard in the world. Males grow longer and heavier than a man.

Mammals That Lay Eggs

Some of the strangest of all animals live on the island continent of Australia. Perhaps the weirdest is the platypus—a furry mammal with a beak and webbed feet like a duck's. Even stranger is its habit of laying eggs. Spiny anteaters from Australia and New Guinea are the only other mammals that lay eggs instead of giving birth to babies.

Pouched Mammals

Most Australian mammals are marsupials. Their name comes from the mother's *marsupium* or belly pouch where her tiny babies live and grow once they are born. When it is born, a red

The platypus looks so strange that experts did not believe descriptions of this mammal until they saw one for themselves.

kangaroo is smaller than a man's thumb, although it will grow as big as a man.

Some Australian marsupials look surprisingly like some un-pouched mammals that live on other continents. For instance there are marsupial mice, moles, rabbits, and bears.

These marsupials look like the other mammals because both kinds have bodies suited to the same way of life, for instance as burrowers or as tree climbers.

Giants of the Land

Elephants are the largest land animals alive. African elephants like those shown here are even larger than Indian elephants, the only other kind. An African elephant may stand twice as tall as a man and weigh as much as a truck. The largest elephants weigh over six tonnes. This is more than half as heavy again as the heaviest hippopotamus or rhinoceros—the next largest land animals.

An elephant eats grass, leaves and even branches. It grasps them in its trunk and uses this like a hand to bring food to its mouth. An elephant also uses its trunk to suck up dust or water, which it then squirts over its body, much

as people take a shower. Tame Indian elephants are trained to lift heavy logs with their trunks.

Few animals dare attack an elephant. Its hide is tough and difficult to pierce. A threatened elephant can also trample an enemy to death or spear it on its tusks.

An Elephant's Life
After a female elephant has mated, 22 months go by before she gives birth to a baby. A newborn elephant stands only one metre high but weighs more than most men. Twenty years pass before it is full grown. An elephant may live to be seventy. New grinding teeth keep appearing as old ones get worn down. But when at last no teeth remain, the elephant cannot chew its food and it starves to death.

Wonderful Wings

Most land animals move forward by pushing against the ground with limbs that act as levers. In a similar way birds use their wings to travel through the air. Birds' wings are one of nature's most astonishing inventions.

Wings and Feathers

Each wing is made of many feathers. If one or two feathers break, the wing still works. In time its feathers get worn and rubbed. But at least once a year new feathers grow to take their place. Feathers grow from the skin stretched over the arm, wrist, and finger bones. These form the struts that give the wing support. The

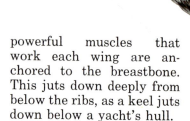

powerful muscles that work each wing are anchored to the breastbone. This juts down deeply from below the ribs, as a keel juts down below a yacht's hull.

Birds can fly because their wings are light but strong, and they have light hollow bones and powerful muscles.

Most birds flap their wings to fly. As the wings move up and down the tips twist around and push air backward. This drives the bird forward.

When a flying great tit lifts its wings the primary feathers open and pass quickly through the air. But when the wings flap down again the feathers close up to push air down and back.

Long outer wing feathers let an Andean condor fly slowly without falling, and soar in tight circles.

Wings are curved on top and flattish below. As they move forward air rushes faster and farther over the top than underneath. So the air above is thinner than the air below, and the wings get sucked and pushed up. This gives a bird the lift it needs to stay up in the air.

Wing Shapes

Ducks and pheasants have short broad wings, which produce enough lift for a quick steep take-off.

Swifts have slim, pointed wings suitable for flying fast with sudden turns. The spine-tailed swift is the fastest animal alive.

Long, narrow wings help an albatross to glide above the sea for weeks on end.

The broad, long wings of eagles and vultures are shaped for soaring high on rising currents of warm air.

59

Birds that Cannot Fly

Some birds have wings too weak for flying. They must find food and escape enemies without taking to the air. Several kinds live on land, others live mainly in the sea.

Most of the flightless birds that live on land are big and run almost as quickly as a horse can gallop. Their size and speed help protect them from most enemies.

The ostrich of Africa is the largest living bird. A male ostrich is much taller and heavier than a man. If cornered an ostrich kicks out dangerously and its claws can rip open a lion. The emu of Australia and the rhea of South America are built much like an ostrich but are smaller. The cassowaries of Australia and New Guinea are stocky, powerful birds. They attack feet first and can kill a man.

The kiwi of New Zealand is a shy forest bird, no larger than a chicken.

Penguins

Penguins use their wings as oars to row them through the sea. They swim well and catch fish and squid.

Most kinds live in cool southern oceans. If a leopard seal attacks them they can leap ashore like corks fired from a popgun.

An emperor penguin and its chick. A penguin's wings are useless for flying, but in the ocean they make splendid oars.

Above: The kiwi lays a
larger egg for its size than
any other bird. Beak-tip
nostrils help kiwis to hunt
worms.

The rhea is shorter and
lighter than a man but it
can outrun a horse. Rheas
roam grasslands in southern
South America.

Water Animals

Water covers nearly three quarters of the Earth. Most of the water is the salty water of the oceans. But fresh water fills thousands of rivers, lakes and pools.

Fresh and salty water are homes to different groups of animals. Some lead lives as strange and interesting as the lives of any animals that stay on land. This chapter looks at water creatures.

Life in Fresh Water
Just like a field or wood, a pond or river is a community of plants and animals.

The smallest creatures are so tiny that you need a microscope to see them. So..e look like little slippers fringed with hairs. Others seem to be just specks of jelly. Different kinds crawl, spin and whizz around to find and feed on tiny water plants or other food.

Moving up the size scale we come to larger but still tiny creatures such as water fleas. If you peer into a pond you may see crowds of these tiny relatives of the crabs and shrimps, jigging jerkily below the surface. Many

small fishes eat animals like these. Small fishes in their turn are gobbled up by larger ones such as pike.

The Part-timers

The creatures already mentioned breathe the air dissolved in water. But ducks, frogs, newts, water spiders, and water beetles spend only part of the time under water. All of them must come up to breathe.

Swimming ducks hold their breath to up-end or dive in search of food.

Frogs and newts start life as tadpoles breathing air dissolved in water. But adult frogs and newts breathe ordinary air and many enter ponds only to lay their eggs. Yet frogs can hibernate under water without drowning.

Water spiders collect air at the surface. Then they swim down to take air bubbles to keep in their underwater nests.

Creatures that live or breed in ponds:
(1) pintail duck
(2) common frog
(3) pond skater
(4) water beetle
(5) male warty newt
(6) female warty newt
(7) water scorpion
(8) water spider diving to its air-filled underwater home.

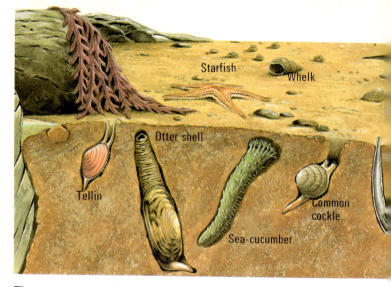

Starfish

Whelk

Otter shell

Tellin

Common cockle

Sea-cucumber

Beneath the Sands

Millions of animals lie hidden below the surface of a sandy beach. Burrowing helps these small sea creatures to stay moist when the tide goes out. They remain safe when storm waves crash above, and whatever the weather they stay comfortably cool.

Some never leave their burrows. A lugworm gulps in sand containing tiny scraps of dead plants and animals. Its body removes this nourishment. Then the lugworm's hind end squirts the used sand up onto the beach in a little pile.

Worm-like sea cucumbers also scavenge in the sands. Each of these relatives of the starfish has a ring of tiny tube feet around one end. The tube feet pull food into the creature's mouth. If another animal grabs the sea cucumber, its body breaks off from the head end. Later the head will grow another body.

Food from Above

At high tide many burrowers collect food from the surface of the beach. Some of them are tube worms living in slime-lined holes in the sand. A crown of

Parchment
worm

Razor
shell

Graham
Allen

Most creatures of this sandy shore live below the surface to avoid enemies and rough seas.

tentacles sprouts from each worm's head. At high tide the tentacles writhe around on the surface and pick up scraps of food.

The tellin feeds differently. (Tellins are bivalves: molluscs with a shell in two hinged halves.) At high tide, tellins use a kind of vacuum tube to suck food off the beach.

Tellins and some other bivalves also suck in water at high tide and sift out the tiny animals and plants carried by it. Otter shells always stay deeply buried and suck in water through a long, hard tube. Cockles and razor shells climb up through the sand to feed at high tide, then burrow again. Cockles have thick, ribbed shells that grip the sand. Razor shells have thin, smooth shells. They would be easily dislodged by storms or birds unless they burrowed deeply. A razor shell can plunge down through the sand faster than a man can dig.

Hidden Hunters
Worms and molluscs living in the sands fall prey to hunters also hiding there.

One hunter is the necklace shell. This sea snail makes holes in the bivalves' shells and sucks them dry.

Several kinds of fishes hunt and hide among the sands. The small, blunt-headed sandy gobies dart about in shallow pools.

Young plaice, whose bodies are the same colour as the sand, watch for shrimps and tube worms.

Slim sand eels swim inshore and snap up worms and baby fishes. Sand eels can use their long lower jaws as shovels to dig themselves into the sand and hide from their prey.

65

Life on the Rocks

Sea creatures living on a rocky shore can cling to rocks or swim in pools that hold water even at low tide. But storm waves, sun and chilly winds attack animals that live on rocks left bare when the tide falls. Rock pools heat up and cool down quickly, and sometimes heavy rain makes their salty water almost fresh.

Periwinkles

Mussels

Bristle worm

Sea urchin

Barnacles

Scallop

Sea anemone

Peacock worm

In a Rock Pool

Seaweed and crevices in rock pools provide hiding places for crustaceans like prawns and shore crabs. Here, too, certain bristle worms swim and creep about. Pools with floors of muddy gravel can be homes to peacock worms that push out feathery tentacles to fish for food in the water.

Sea urchins move about on scores of tube feet that poke out through tiny holes in the prickly cases that guard their soft bodies.

Sea anemones' rubbery bodies cling to the rocks. At high tide, the anemones' tentacles catch small creatures passing by. At low tide sea anemones left high and dry close up like buds.

Life at Low Tide

When the tide drops, crabs and worms can creep into damp crevices. But creatures that are fixed to the rocks must find other ways of staying moist.

Some sea anemones produce a slimy substance that stops them drying out. Acorn barnacles close up. Limpets press their shells against the rock. Top-shells and periwinkles cover the mouths of their shells with a tough, waterproof 'skin'.

A periwinkle stranded on dry land can live for months, breathing air with a special kind of lung.

Rock pool creatures have different ways of surviving when storm waves burst in. Mussels have threads to tether them to the rock. Piddocks bore holes.

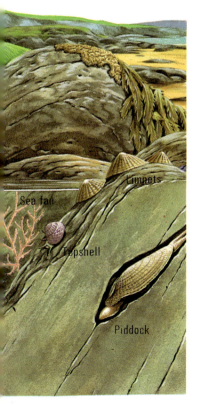

Sea fan

Limpets

Topshell

Piddock

Ocean Drifters

Countless millions of tiny, drifting plants and animals live in the oceans. These drifters are called plankton.

The left-hand column below shows some plankton plants, much larger than in real life. The plants in glassy boxes are called *diatoms*. The 'anchor' and the 'Chinese hat' are plants called *dinoflagellates*. Plankton plants all live in the surface waters, where there is enough sunlight for the plants to use to make food.

The spiky organisms in the right-hand column below are tiny plankton animals called *radiolarians*. The spikes help to spread their weight and stop them sinking. The third column shows crustaceans much enlarged. The top one is a

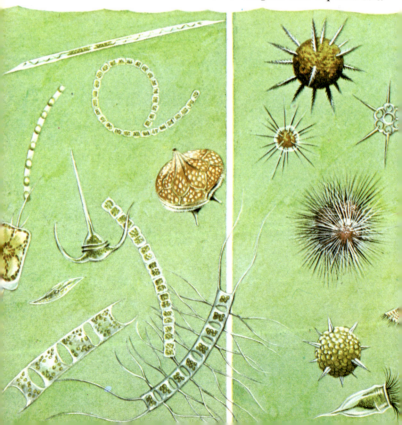

full-grown copepod. The spiky one below it is a baby crab; when it is full grown it will live on the sea bed. The creatures in the fourth column are marine worms. Some have little paddles to help them swim.

Sea Soup
In cool seas plankton can breed astonishingly fast. In just one month a diatom may produce 100 million descendants. This is just as well, for small plankton animals eat enormous numbers of plankton plants. For example, a copepod almost too small to be seen can eat 120,000 diatoms in a day. Larger plankton animals eat the smaller ones.

   Almost all creatures in the sea depend in some way upon the plant or animal plankton for food. Together, they make seawater a weak, nourishing broth.

Creatures of the Deep

The strangest ocean creatures are fishes living deep down, where it is always cold and dark. Here, food is too scarce to satisfy large fishes and most deep-sea kinds are smaller than a person's hand.

Yet many deep-sea fishes look terrifying. They have sharp teeth, gaping jaws and stomachs like elastic bags. All this helps them to eat the few large meals that come their way. Fishes called gulpers and swallowers can even bolt down creatures that are larger than themselves.

To save energy, angler fishes and some others wait in ambush for their prey. Each tiny male angler lives glued to a female angler, who can be half a million times larger than he is.

Living Lights

The anglers attract their victims by waving fleshy lures that glow with light that is produced by certain chemicals.

Some deep-sea fishes have rows of lights running down their bodies. These lights may help the fishes to find mates. A deep-sea fish can also flash its lights quickly on and off to confuse an enemy. Some fishes have huge eyes to help them see the lights of others.

Left: Three deep-sea fishes. They are (1) *Eustomias*; (2) *Astronesthes*; (3) angler fish. All have lighted lures to attract prey. Two have rows of body lights. On the right is a deep-sea squid.

Ocean Dangers

Four dangers that lurk in tropical seas. The clam may crush, and the eel bites. The scorpion fish and sea urchin have sharp, poisonous spines to protect them.

Among the hunters and the hunted creatures of the seas are some with powerful weapons of attack or defence.

People swimming in warm oceans fear sharks more than any other dangers. Killers like the great white

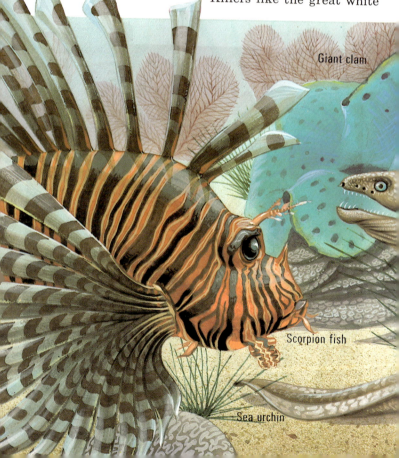

Giant clam.

Scorpion fish

Sea urchin

shark have overlapping rows of hard sharp teeth. One bite can chop off someone's leg.

Sharks largely hunt by smell, and are attracted by the smell of blood. If one shark in a group is wounded, the rest will set upon it and kill their fellow creature.

Barracudas are slim fishes shorter than a man, but they can be just as dangerous as a much larger shark. A shoal of these aggressive hunters may attack in only knee-deep water, and their powerful jaws bristle with teeth as sharp as razors.

Hidden Risks

Some hunters are less obviously dangerous. Jellyfish drift along harmlessly enough—until an animal brushes by their tentacles. Then the animal is hit and paralyzed by poisoned threads.

Moray eels hide in rocky crevices. A diver who puts his hand in such a crevice may have it bitten off.

Tales are told of divers who have drowned when giant clams trapped their feet. Yet clams only shut their shells in defence, so accidents like this are most unlikely. But divers in warm seas have died because they trod upon a fish protected by sharp, poisoned spines.

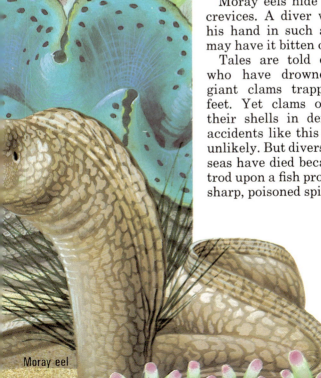

Moray eel

Ocean Giants

Whales are descended from land mammals that took up life in the sea. With water to help to hold up their bodies, some kinds of whale have grown larger than any creature now living on land.

Largest of all is the blue whale. One captured blue whale measured over 29 metres, equal to a line of eight family cars; and it weighed 177 tonnes, or as much as 366 riding horses.

Whales are almost as well built for swimming as fishes. Most have stream-lined bodies.

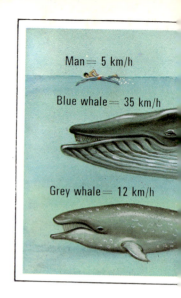

Man = 5 km/h

Blue whale = 35 km/h

Grey whale = 12 km/h

Killer whale

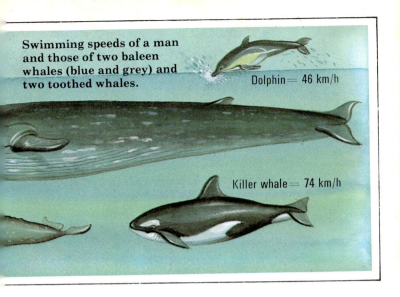

Swimming speeds of a man and those of two baleen whales (blue and grey) and two toothed whales.

Dolphin = 46 km/h

Killer whale = 74 km/h

A whale's front legs have become flippers that help it to brake and steer. Two tail flukes flattened from above and below help the animal to dive, and to drive its body through the water.

Thick fat called blubber keeps out the cold. Unlike a fish a whale must come up to the surface to breathe. But some whales can stay under water for more than an hour.

Baleen Whales
There are two groups of whales: baleen and toothed whales. Most of the largest are baleen whales. They feed by swimming with open mouths, and sucking in water holding millions of tiny shrimp-like creatures called krill. When the whale squirts out water the krill are trapped by the baleen plates hanging from the roof of its mouth.

Toothed Whales
Toothed whales include the killer whale, dolphins, and the much larger sperm whale. Sperm whales will dive 1000 metres to feed on squid, and probably three times as deep to hunt sea bed sharks. A pack of killer whales can kill a baleen whale far larger than its attackers.

Surprising Facts

Powerful Poisons

Bees, wasps, spiders, many snakes and some other animals kill enemies by poison. These pages describe animals whose poisons are deadly to man.

Fatal Frogs

The colourful arrow-poison frogs have skins poisonous enough to kill any beasts that bite them. As little as 1/100,000th of a gramme of poison from one species of arrow-poison frog could kill a man. No other animal venom is so powerful.

Forest Indians of tropical America tip their hunting darts and arrows with this venom.

Stung by Scorpions

Scorpions are eight-legged relatives of spiders. They seize prey with

pincers and sting with poison stored in the tip of the tail. Some scorpions are deadly. One kind killed nearly 400 people in Algeria in 14 years. In Mexico and the United States, more people die from scorpion stings than from snake-bites.

Australian funnel-web spiders and certain others can kill human beings. Among insects the bite of a black bulldog ant can be lethal.

Death by Snakebite

Poisonous snakes kill more than 40,000 people a year. Three-quarters of these deaths are in India where king cobras kill the most.

The most poisonous land snake is Australia's small-scaled snake. One specimen may hold enough venom to kill dozens of people. Even that snake is far less deadly than one kind of sea snake. Luckily this species very rarely bites swimmers.

Clever Animals

Certain animals are particularly clever at performing some kind of difficult task. Many are born with an instinct that tells them what to do. Some are intelligent enough to be taught.

A Tool-using Finch
Scientists once thought only people made tools. We now know that several animals do this. Among these is the woodpecker finch of the Galápagos Islands off South America. This small bird chooses a cactus spine. It nips off any unwanted piece. Gripping one end of the spine in its beak, it uses the other end to probe cracks and crevices for wood-boring grubs.

Dolphin Acrobats
Captive dolphins kept in oceanariums enjoy learning acrobatic tricks. Their

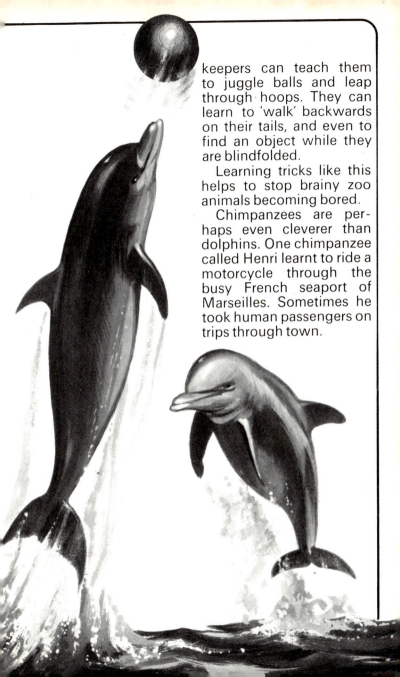

keepers can teach them to juggle balls and leap through hoops. They can learn to 'walk' backwards on their tails, and even to find an object while they are blindfolded.

Learning tricks like this helps to stop brainy zoo animals becoming bored.

Chimpanzees are perhaps even cleverer than dolphins. One chimpanzee called Henri learnt to ride a motorcycle through the busy French seaport of Marseilles. Sometimes he took human passengers on trips through town.

Useful Animals

Guanay cormorant

Animals have always served man in one way or another. At first man hunted wild beasts for food. Later he tamed and raised cattle and other farm animals for their meat, milk and hides. He also learnt to use certain creatures in unusual ways.

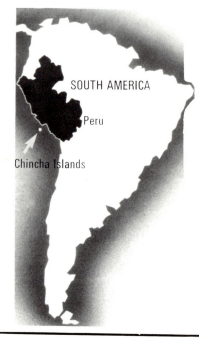

SOUTH AMERICA

Peru

Chincha Islands

Farmers' Friends
Dried seabirds' droppings are a valuable fertilizer. In 27 years, workers gathered about 20 million tonnes from islands off Peru, called the Chincha Islands. Much of this *guano* came from millions of guanay cormorants.

Animal Fishermen

Some Chinese and Japanese fishermen let captive cormorants do their work for them. Each bird dives off a fishing boat and catches a fish. But a line attaching the bird to the boat stops it from escaping, and a leather collar prevents it swallowing its catch. The fisherman hauls the bird up and takes the fish from its beak.

Some fishermen in warm seas catch turtles, using a line tied to a remora. This fish uses its sucker to fasten onto any large creature to hitch itself a ride.

Wealth from a Whale

A smelly black substance called ambergris forms inside a sperm whale's intestines. The whale spits this ambergris out and it floats in the sea. Sunshine and air turn it pale and give it a delicate scent.

When manufacturers mix ambergris with other ingredients it helps produce long-lasting perfumes. This makes ambergris very valuable. Early this century one large lump was sold for as much as a small street of houses.

Insect Allies

Man's best-known insect friends are the honeybee and the silkworm. In order to change into a moth, the silkworm spins a cocoon around itself. This cocoon is made of strands of silk, which we weave into silk cloth.

Less well known are two useful scale insects. One kind lives in Mexico. The insects' dried, crushed bodies yield the crimson dye cochineal, which is used to colour sweets and cosmetics.

Shellac is a resin used in polishes and varnishes. It comes from an Asian scale insect.

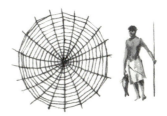

Papuan Fisherman

A Spider Surprise

One New Guinea spider weaves a web 2·4 metres across. Papuan fishermen gather the webs with looped sticks and use them as fishing nets.

Extinct Animals

Only a fraction of all the kinds of animal that ever lived are still alive today. Most died off long ago when their surroundings changed in ways their bodies could not stand. But in the last 20,000 years many animals have been wiped out by man.

Vanished Giants

Dinosaurs died out long before man evolved. But, for more than 100 million years, dinosaurs larger than the largest living elephant roamed most continents. *Stegosaurus*, shown below, weighed 8·5 tonnes. *Brachiosaurus*

was nearly 12 times heavier than that. But *Brachiosaurus* weighed less than half as much as a dinosaur nicknamed '*Supersaurus*'. This 250-tonne monster was the largest land animal ever.

Disappearing Dodos
In 1598 sailors crossing the Indian Ocean discovered strange birds living on the island of Mauritius. They were larger than a turkey but had tiny wings and could not fly. This

Dodo

made them easy to catch and kill. The Portuguese called them *doudo*, meaning 'simpleton'. From this word came the birds' English name of dodo.

But as the name caught on the birds were dying out. Less than a century after its discovery, the dodo was killed off by human settlers and the dogs and rats that landed with them. Not even a stuffed dodo survives.

No More Pigeon Pie
In the early 1800s the passenger pigeon of North America was the most plentiful bird in the world. Yet by 1914 hunters, and farmers felling forests had wiped it out.

Endangered Animals

Endangered Animals
Hunting, felling forests and other human acts are making many creatures scarcer. By 1980, over 1000 species and subspecies of backboned animal were threatened. One million species of animal and plant may have disappeared by the year 2000.

Raptors at Risk
Raptors (birds of prey) are becoming rarer. One of the rarest is the California condor of southern California. Only a few dozen of these huge vultures still soar over the mountains.

California condor

Tiger Tragedies
Outside zoos, wild tigers are becoming very scarce. One rare kind, on the Indo-

Caspian tiger

84

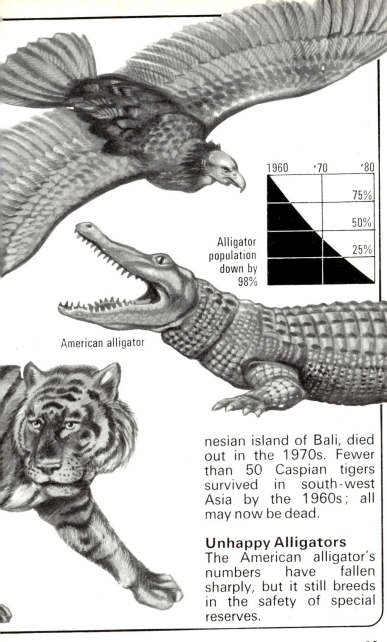

1960　　'70　　'80

		75%
		50%
		25%

Alligator
population
down by
98%

American alligator

nesian island of Bali, died
out in the 1970s. Fewer
than 50 Caspian tigers
survived in south-west
Asia by the 1960s; all
may now be dead.

Unhappy Alligators

The American alligator's
numbers have fallen
sharply, but it still breeds
in the safety of special
reserves.

Mythical Animals

Before the world was explored, people had no true idea of most of its animals. Rumours and travellers' tales gave rise to stories of weird and terrible animals.

Sea Serpents

Legends told of ships seized by giant snakes with dragon's heads. In the 1800s some ships' crews described seeing sea serpents as long as whales.

So huge and deep are the oceans that strange monsters may truly lurk in their depths. But most scientists believe that the 'sea serpents' seen were animals such as giant squids, low-flying birds, leaping porpoises or oar-fish. These can be 15 metres long, with a ribbon-like body, a head like a horse's and a flaming red mane of fins.

The Unicorn

The unicorn of old myths was a horse-like beast with a long straight horn growing from its forehead.

The real 'unicorn' was probably the Arabian oryx. This big antelope has two, long, straight horns. Travellers seeing an oryx from far off could have believed that it had one horn instead of a pair.

The Firebird

In Greek myth, the phoenix was a bird that lived 500 years, then burnt itself on a fire. From the ashes a new young phoenix arose.

Perhaps this legend came from a habit called 'anting'. Crows, starlings and some other birds place crushed ants under their wings. Formic acid produced by the crushed ants may kill parasites that bother the birds.

One pet bird anted by holding its wings close to a lighted match. Birds that anted in the embers of a dying fire may have led to the phoenix legend.

Fake Animals

Jokers and tricksters used to fake monsters by sticking together bits of different beasts. Ignorant people believed that the fakes were real and paid to see them.

Mermaids

Creatures supposed to be half human and half fish amazed visitors to some museums in the 1800s. In 1875 the naturalist Frank Buckland described the mermaid shown above. The head end was probably from a monkey and the tail end came from a carp-like fish.

A Many-Headed Monster

Greek myths describe many-headed monsters called hydras. In the early 1700s a Hamburg merchant claimed to have one, dead and stuffed. Visitors were astonished by this snake-like beast with seven heads, two legs and a scaly tail. King Frederick IV of Denmark supposedly offered a fortune for it, but the German owner refused to sell.

Then the Swedish naturalist Carl Linnaeus took a close look at the man-length creature. He quickly saw it had weasels' heads and feet, and snakes' skins pasted on the body.

Linnaeus rightly guessed the thing was a model of a dragon mentioned in the Bible. Its makers had been monks, and the model once stood on a church altar in the city of Prague.

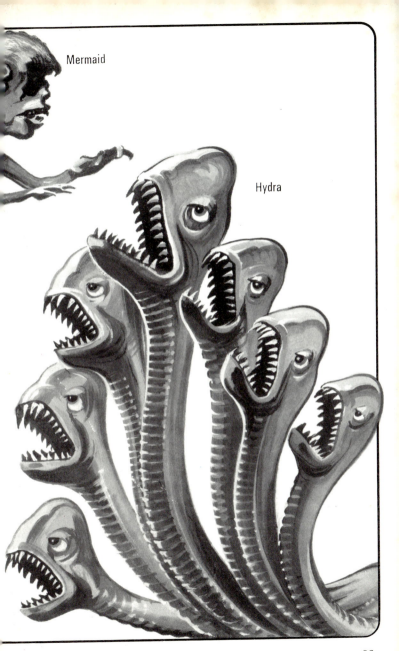

Mermaid

Hydra

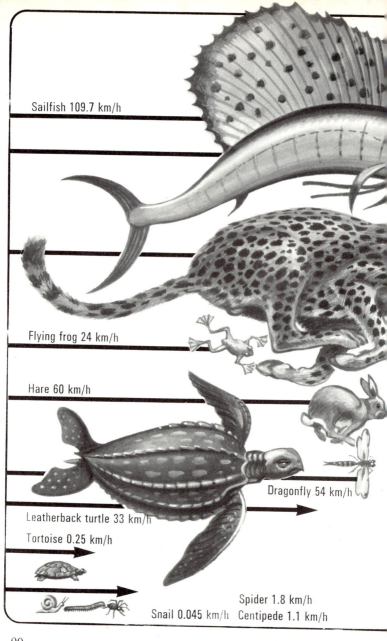

Sailfish 109.7 km/h

Flying frog 24 km/h

Hare 60 km/h

Dragonfly 54 km/h

Leatherback turtle 33 km/h

Tortoise 0.25 km/h

Spider 1.8 km/h

Snail 0.045 km/h Centipede 1.1 km/h

The Tortoise and The Hare

A famous fable tells how a tortoise outraced a hare. Hares can run 264 times faster than tortoises. These pages show how fast various kinds of creatures move.

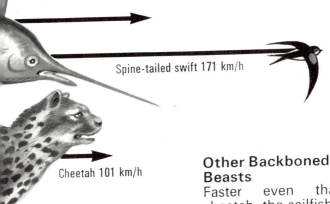

Spine-tailed swift 171 km/h

Cheetah 101 km/h

Fast and Slow Mammals

The fastest mammal is the cheetah. Perhaps the slowest is the sloth. A cheetah at full gallop moves more than 46 times faster than a sloth is known to crawl.

Bird Record Holders

At up to 171 km/h the spine-tailed swift is possibly the fastest bird and indeed the fastest animal of any kind. The slowest birds are soaring birds like eagles, and gliders like albatrosses. An albatross can hang in the air that rushes up a cliff face.

Other Backboned Beasts

Faster even than a cheetah, the sailfish is the fastest of all cold-blooded animals that have a backbone.

Sailfish swim more than three times faster than leatherback turtles, the fastest reptiles. The fastest amphibians are flying frogs; but these glide from tree to tree more slowly than the leatherbacks can swim.

Invertebrates

Dragonflies are probably the fastest animals without a backbone. Flying at 54 km/h a dragonfly zooms along 1200 times faster than a garden snail can crawl.

INDEX

Page numbers in *italics* refer to illustrations.